# Listen, Buddy

WITHDRAWN

## Helen Lester
## Illustrated by Lynn Munsinger

Houghton Mifflin Harcourt
Boston    New York    2013

For more information on the importance of listening skills and to download a free version of this story, visit www.hmhbooks.com/freedownloads/.

Access code: goodlistening

To Lenesa — Thanks for listening.
H.L.

Text copyright © 1995 by Helen Lester
Illustrations copyright © 1995 by Lynn Munsinger

HMH Books is an imprint of Houghton Mifflin Harcourt Publishing Company.

www.hmhbooks.com

The text of this book is set in Adobe Garamond Pro.

Library of Congress Catalog Control Number 94-33634

ISBN 978-0-544-00322-4
Manufactured in China
SCP 10 9 8 7 6 5 4 3 2 1
4500406234

Buddy's father had a beautiful big nose.
He was a great sniffer.

Buddy's mother had beautiful big teeth.
She was a great chomper.

Buddy had beautiful big ears.

It didn't matter.

When Buddy's parents sent him to the vegetable stand to get
a basket of squash, he came home with a basket of wash.

When they asked him to buy fifteen tomatoes, he
came home with fifty potatoes.

Buddy's father said, "Listen, Buddy, will you please
bring me a pen?"
"Who?" asked Buddy.
"You," said his father.
"Will you please bring me a pen?"
"A what?" asked Buddy.

"A pen," said his father.
"Will you please bring me a pen?"
"Sure," said Buddy.
Buddy's father said, "Listen, Buddy!"

Buddy's mother said, "Listen, Buddy, will you please
get me a slice of bread?"
"Who?" asked Buddy.
"You," said his mother. "Will you please get me
a slice of bread?"
"A what of what?" asked Buddy.

"A slice of bread," said his mother. "Will you please bring me a slice of bread?"
"Sure," said Buddy.
Buddy's mother said, "Listen, Buddy!"

Somehow Buddy's mind was always wandering too far
away from those beautiful ears.
His parents tried yelling. "LISTEN, BUDDY!"

They tried whispering. "Listen, Buddy."
Nothing worked.

One day Buddy got permission to go for a long hop.
He had never before been allowed to go beyond
the vegetable stand.

"Listen, Buddy," his parents warned him. "Just remember
that at the end of the road, there are two paths.
The path to the left will lead you around the pond and
back home. But the path to the right will lead you
to the cave of the Scruffy Varmint. And that
Scruffy Varmint has a nasty temper, so be sure to
take the path to the left."

"Right?" asked Buddy.

"Left," said his parents.

"Right!" said Buddy. And with a salute of his paw
he hopped away.

Feeling very grown up, Buddy hopped along, past the
vegetable stand and on to the end of the road.
"Now let's see," he pondered. "Was I supposed to go
left or right?
Or right?
Or left?"

He thought as hard as he could.
"The last thing I said was 'Right!' so that must be . . . right."
Right he went.

Twenty-five hops later, Buddy discovered that right
was wrong. There in front of his cave was the
Scruffy Varmint, doing scruffy things that varmints do, like
snarling, mussing his hair, rubbing dirt on his knees,
and scratching a whole lot of itches. At his feet
was a large soup pot.

"What are you going to do with that soup pot?"
asked Buddy.

"What does one usually do with a soup pot — bake pie?"
replied the Scruffy Varmint, not too kindly.

"I'm going to make some soup."

"Some what?" asked Buddy.

"Soup," snarled the Scruffy Varmint.

Buddy had forgotten his parents' warning about the
Scruffy Varmint. He asked eagerly, "May I help?"
The Scruffy Varmint was not fond of having company, but
with help he'd have his soup sooner, so he said, "Alllll
right, Bunnyrabbit, come help me gather firewood."
"Who, what?" asked Buddy.
"You. Firewood."
Buddy eagerly hopped ahead of the Scruffy Varmint.
Very gently he gathered a large prickly bundle,
which he held out proudly.

Roughly the Varmint grabbed the bundle. "I said
firewood, not briarwood," he yelped, plucking the
sharp thorns from his paws.

Later, when the pot was filled with water, the
Scruffy Varmint lay against a rock, licking his paws
and barking orders.

"Hustle, Bunnyrabbit. Get the flour."

"Yessir!" said Buddy.

"Five pinches of salt."
"Yessir!" said Buddy.
"Fifteen tomatoes."
"Yessir!" said Buddy.

"And a big load of squash."

"Yessir!" said Bunny.

The Scruffy Varmint rose and gave the soup a stir.

He took a taste. It tasted a little like . . . well,

a little . . . maybe it needed some pepper.

"Bunnyrabbit, get the pepper from the left side of the kitchen sink," the Varmint growled.

"Who get the what from the where side of the where what?" asked Buddy.

The Scruffy Varmint repeated, "WHO GET THE WHAT FROM
THE WHERE SIDE OF THE WHERE WHAT? Never mind."
He stalked into the kitchen and got the pepper
himself and sprinkled it into the soup.
"There," he snarled. "Now, Bunnyrabbit, put the
soup on the fire."

Buddy put the soup *in* the fire.

The fire went Hsssssssss.
So did the Scruffy Varmint.
"I'll teach you," he howled. "I WILL have soup!
Bunnyrabbit soup! And I know just the bunny to use,
the Bunnyrabbit who never listens!"
Buddy listened.

He also hopped.
Veryveryvery fast.
Faster than he had ever hopped in his life.

He whizzed up the road past the vegetable stand and into the safety of his house.

And a little later, when Buddy's parents asked him
to bring a pen and a slice of bread,
Buddy listened.